OMEGA'S POSSESSIVE ALPHA

MPREG Wolf Shifter Romance

Michael Levi

CONTENTS

CHAPTER 1

Look, it didn't really matter how much my father wanted to make this happen, it wasn't going to. Even though the party was energetic, it wasn't going to make me fall for the cocky guy standing across from me all the way on the other side of the main hall.

"He's just so much older than me. There is no way that there can ever be a relationship between us," I said to my best friend. Draco was standing here with me and he was a member of the pack.

Even though I would never say this, the truth was that I would rather be in a romantic relationship with him than with Lux. I mean, it just wouldn't really work.

Although, I couldn't help but admit that he was quite the eye candy. He was fit. His body was sculpted, his muscles showing even though he was wearing a dark suit. It didn't really fit him, though. I just had no idea what he even thought he was doing here at this party.

"Does age really matter that much? I mean, he is only 30 years old and you are 21. It's about time you started to go to college or just do something with your life. I'm in college, and I really enjoy it."

Draco tried to smile, but he wasn't really fooling anyone here.

He didn't actually enjoy attending classes and whatever else he thought he was doing in college. As for me, my career was focused on something else. I was focused on becoming a developer. A programmer. That was what I was focused on and nothing would change that.

I took a sip from the wineglass I was holding. Grimacing, I just really couldn't understand why people thought that wine tasted good. It just didn't.

"It matters to me. I'm not going to begin a relationship with anyone just because my father wants it. Not to mention that he still thinks there is something as ridiculous as 'fated mates.' Just thinking about it, I feel like I'm going to puke."

And yet, my eyes couldn't stop glancing to the left and stealing glances at him. I had no idea what I was even doing. If Lux noticed that I was stealing glances at him, he would certainly take the next step and come to me.

"I just think that you are wrong about this. You should go and talk to him at least. It can't really hurt," he said as he winked. I rolled my eyes and then began to walk away. Where to? I didn't know. Anywhere that wasn't the main hall was good enough for me.

In a moment, I found myself outside, and here I could breathe and think about everything going on in my life. There was this pressure on me to marry and find my partner, even though it was ridiculous.

I sat down on a chair by the swimming pool. I couldn't deny that I was spoiled. My house was more like a mansion. It was big and fancy, and I knew a lot of people would give almost everything they had to live the rest of their lives here.

At least, that was what I was telling myself anyway. I was just trying to make myself feel better about my current, shitty situation.

The air around me was fresh and calming. I inhaled it slowly while still thinking about Lux. What was about him that kept on making my mind go back to him all the time?

Maybe it was his impossibly blue eyes and his manly scent. I was an Omega, so I could smell him without difficulty even from a distance, just like now. Even though he was still in the main hall, I could smell him. And it was really like he was right behind me.

"I saw you coming here," his voice echoed behind me. I shot up from where I was sitting while whirling around and meeting his eyes as they continued to stare at me. I never thought that he would show up all of a sudden when I was trying to think about anything that didn't involve him.

"What are you doing here?" I asked as I raised my voice. It was like I was begging for someone to help me. Maybe Draco would come, but I didn't think so. He was probably mingling with the other partygoers right now.

"I needed some fresh air, so I came outside. Nothing more than that, really. It certainly doesn't mean that I wanted to talk to you in person." He smirked after saying that. Of course he was going to do that. Lux was so convinced about the effect he was having on me.

I took a few steps away from him. He wasn't going to fool me now no matter what happened.

"Stay away from me!" I shouted. This time, I did that while hoping that at least one of the partygoers would hear it. Whether that would happen or not, we were going to find out in the next couple of seconds.

But… There was only gentle music coming from the main hall. Nobody heard anything, which made me feel even more paralyzed than I was right now.

My cock was hard. There was no denying it. If there was something I wanted to make happen right now, it was this Alpha manhandling me the way that I knew he could. He would put me right back in my place and then he would kiss me. I could just imagine how soft his lips were.

But I shouldn't even be thinking that. He could read my mind. I was certain he could do that.

He lifted his hands and put them in front of him as though he was making a stop sign. "All right, all right. You don't need to worry about that. I'm not going to do anything to you that you don't want."

After a moment of silence, I realized that he wasn't going to harm me or try to touch me without my consent. Where was everybody? I asked myself, realizing how stupid I was being about this. The truth was that I was still in my house and, given that, Lux had to get out of here if I said so to the guards.

His hands were in his pockets, and this was the first time he looked so not threatening. It was different from what I was used to.

"When we first met, you told me that you didn't like me at all. I didn't do anything against you, so I'm wondering why you said that even though we don't actually know each other properly yet."

I took a deep breath in, taking a couple of steps toward the swimming pool. What was I thinking I was doing? I had no idea, but I still wanted to put as much distance between us as possible.

"You are a biker. You are a member of the Alpha MC and if there is something I hate, it's bikes. They are terrible, loud, and greasy."

He chuckled. "Why is that?"

"It's pretty obvious, isn't it? I only drive cars."

"That's a very stupid reason to hate motorcycles."

"Well, it's my reason to think about it that way, and there is nothing about it you can do to change my mind."

He took a step toward me and I didn't move. Lux wasn't suddenly going to kiss me and sweep me up in his arms. It didn't matter how much I wanted to make that happen, it just never would. I could see it in his eyes. Even though he was a biker, he respected my decisions.

"Is that a challenge?" He taunted.

I gulped. I never thought that he would throw that back at me so swiftly. He knew what he was doing, no denying it. He knew how to put me against a wall that didn't even exist.

"Of course not. I would never say it's a challenge."

He chuckled again and then took a few more steps toward me. I could see the moon in the sky. It was behind him. It shone brightly around his body, making his eyes stand out. Or maybe I was only imagining things.

"I think it's a challenge. Do you have anything else to say in your defense? Do you want to convince me it's not that?" He asked.

My shaft was just so hard right now. He was putting me in such a submissive position it was difficult for me to climb out of it. Even though part of me didn't want to let me do this, it was smaller than the other part that wanted to make me go along with this.

Why was I so silly like this? I asked myself as I wanted to kick myself so hard right now.

"I don't have to say anything about that," I said when I took another step backward, and then there was no more ground for me to step on. After taking the last step, I fell backward into the swimming pool, and then there was only water surrounding me.

And the worst part about this? It was that I didn't even know how to swim.

CHAPTER 2

Looking at Alix was enough to make my shaft so hard right now, and I wasn't even ashamed of thinking about it this way. Either way, it wasn't like I had much time to do that. Did I know what I was doing? Kind of. I didn't intend for him to fall into the swimming pool. Alix did that without me having to do anything to force it to happen.

I jumped into the water after him. It was the only thing I could do right now, and as I moved my arms in the water, I had just one goal in mind – that of saving him. No matter what happened, I was going to get him out of the water safe and sound.

I swam in the water as fast as I could and since the distance between us was short, it didn't take me long to get to him. One thing I noticed was that Alix didn't know how to swim. He kept on flailing his arms around as he tried to keep himself afloat. It wasn't working, though. The moment when I put my arms around him, he was already falling deeper inside the water, and it didn't look like he was capable of turning things around.

I wrapped my arms around him and then I brought him up and went over the surface of the water. He shook his head as he tried to open his eyes, gasping for air. I moved with him to the edge of the swimming pool, and then I pulled him up until he was on the tiles around it.

After doing that, I came out as well while water drops fell on the tiles. Seconds later, Alix was already regaining his breath and he looked at me with confusion in his eyes. I could already see him blaming me for what happened, even though it was ridiculous. He was the one that was stepping away from me without looking at what was behind him, and especially without remembering that there was a swimming pool there.

His clothes were drenched with water as was his hair. Alix looked cuter now than I had ever seen him before, which made my dick jump under my pants. I shouldn't be feeling this way, but I still was.

"I saved you," I pointed out while standing up slowly and holding out my hand. He had to take it. It was the least he could do as a thank you.

"I don't care about that," he said while rising up on his own.

I chuckled. There was nothing about him that could truly make me like him less.

My eyes scanned his body. Now that his clothes were hugging his curves tightly, it was the first time I could see just how lust-inducing they were. The only thing I wanted to be doing right now, other than going with him to a room where we could be together, was to be running my hands all over his muscles.

It was such a pity that I couldn't do that right now and it was also such a shame that he still hated me so much.

"You're not even going to say you are thankful?"

"As far as I'm concerned, you intended for this to happen from the beginning," he barked at me, and I chuckled again.

"I guess you don't really care that everybody's going to see you so wet."

His cheeks blushed. He didn't think that I was going to make that pun.

"Look, Lux, I don't really care what you're thinking or what you are hoping this is going to lead to, but it's not going to make me change my mind about you. I'm going to my room and I'm going to get dressed, and nobody will notice anything."

"Nobody will notice anything? Don't you think that people

will notice the son of the owner of the house walking around so wet? They might suspect that you were with me, especially because I'm also going inside the house right now."

"You're not going anywhere. You're going to stay right here."

I slipped my hands into my pockets. Even though I really wanted to go inside, I was enjoying this little moment we were having together. It was an argument I never thought I would have with Alix.

"Then what?" I asked, stepping toward him. Even though he still hated me so much, he just couldn't really hide that he thought I was hot. Not many people could do that, I remembered. "You're going to get me a change of clothes?"

"I'm not going to do that. You figure out what you're going to do, but you are definitely not walking back inside with your clothes soaked like that."

I chuckled again. "You do realize that you can't actually force me to do anything, right?"

He opened his mouth to rebuke me, but then he closed it right away. That was exactly what I thought he was going to do. Now that he was soaked with the water, his scent was even stronger than before. It made me want to be just a tiny little bit closer to him so that I could smell it even more than I already was.

"I don't know what I'm going to do and I certainly don't know what you're going to do, but I'm going to my room and I'm going to lock myself in it. If anybody asks for me, I'll just say that I don't want to talk to anybody."

He whirled around when I was going to say that his father was going to be disappointed. After all, he'd set up this party so that we had a chance to get to know each other better, me and Alix.

I did make sure to watch his ass carefully while he ran away from me. He disappeared inside the house, and I heard some people gasping after they noticed him rushing upstairs with heavy footsteps. Even though I was far away from him, I could still hear his heavy footsteps echoing from within the house.

I heard him slamming the door shut and then closing the window, most likely imagining that he wasn't going to see me anymore, both tonight and in all the other days that were going to come after this one.

But that was silly.

I needed a change of clothes right now, and I wasn't going to ask anyone else for that. So, my eyes noticed a path leading upwards to his bedroom, which I took to propel myself all the way there. I wasn't just fit, but my body was also quite nimble.

Also, tonight I wasn't ready to be away from Alix. I needed to talk to him a little more. I felt that we made some good progress.

Without saying anything about it, I positioned myself behind his window and then peered inside. Even though he'd locked it, I could still open it with ease.

However, I wasn't going to do that right now. No point in spooking him when he was changing his clothes. I knew that this was wrong, but c'mon, I was the founder of the Alpha MC and I'd done plenty of wrong in my life already. This was nothing in comparison.

Alix took off his shirt, his pants, and his underwear, right now mumbling to himself. "That fucking jerk made me fall into the water on purpose. I just know he did."

I sighed. He still thought I'd intended on making him look like a fool like that? C'mon. I wasn't that heartless and I wanted to make him like me a little right now.

Nothing more than that.

I kept my lips sealed while he opened the closet. His body was really so sexy. I doubted that he thought that way about it, but truly, everything about him made me want to fuck him so much. Plus, it wasn't like I had much to lose right now...

If he thought that I came to his party to waste my time, then he had something coming.

I opened the window and jumped through it before landing inside his room. He gasped and whirled around while holding a shirt. He covered his junk with it, but it wasn't really helping him with anything, and it was just pointless. I'd already seen him naked and his shaft dangling between his legs.

I wanted it. All of it and nothing was going to stop me now.

Not to mention that his scent had grown even thicker and more intense in the air.

CHAPTER 3

Alix

"What the fuck do you think you're doing in my room?" I barked. I just couldn't believe that he was so audacious. Lux burst inside the room and was now standing no more than a couple of feet from me. I should have remembered to shut the window with the lock.

And yes, I couldn't deny that his presence in my room was stiffening my shaft. I should be feeling ashamed of that, and I was, but it was also kind of good.

"I'm here for my change of clothes, nothing more than that," Lux replied while taking a few steps toward me. Gosh, I just wanted so much to punch him right on his cheek, and it sucked that I couldn't do that. I was an Omega and weak in comparison to him.

"I said I wasn't going to give you any change of clothes."

He folded his arms over his chest, tipping up his chin. "When are you finally going to drop the act?"

I blinked twice. I didn't want to think he meant what I was thinking he did, but he was kind of making me think that was exactly what was going on here.

He knew I had a crush on him, didn't he?

"What are you talking about? I'm not pretending to be doing anything. It's not an act."

"Yeah, it *is* an act. You want to make me think that you don't have the hots for me, but we all know that's not exactly true."

"I want you out of my room. That's exactly what I want right now."

"You are going to have to force me out of your room. I'm not going anywhere. I came here for my change of clothes and I'm going to get it."

There was a moment of silence while I weighed my words. What should I really do so that Lux stopped being such a bother to me even though he made my cock stiff? After all, my boner was exactly what I was trying to hide with the shirt, even though it was barely working. I had a semi right now, and it kept on growing and I knew that soon it would be a full-fledged erection.

He chuckled again. There was something so infuriating about the way he always chuckled. Lux was always so full of himself, and that was putting it mildly.

"I'm going to call the police. You can't stop me from doing that."

"You calling the police or not doesn't really change anything. What matters is that you are hiding something from me that I want to see. I want to know how much longer you can hide that crush you have on me."

I felt heat rising to my cheeks. I never thought he was going to be so blunt, but I also shouldn't have expected otherwise. The truth was that my balls were aching for him, and I suddenly felt this urge to let him get me pregnant. What was I even thinking would happen in that case? That we would live together and I would have his babies and everything would be fine and dandy?

It was ridiculous. The mere thought of having his babies should be disgusting to me, and yet it was having the opposite effect on me right now.

"I don't have a crush on you. I have no idea where you got that from. Every time I've had the opportunity to talk to you, I've always shown you how much I hate you."

"Well, it's really not working. Do you mind lowering the shirt? I want to see what you are hiding. I know that you have a boner right now."

"That's ridiculous. I'm not going to do that. You are making me feel embarrassed. I don't like to be naked in front of other people."

"If you insist so much, then I'm going to do something about that. I'm going to show you that being naked isn't so bad," Lux murmured before putting his fingers under his shirt and then lifting it up. He did it so fast that I didn't even have time to say anything about it. One moment his shirt covered his chest, and then the next it was exposed and my eyes went wide in an instant. His chest was nothing short of marvelous, and the curves and the lines... They made my mouth water, and that was putting it mildly. My jaw dropped.

He chuckled again. Lux was so cocky and I kept on doing everything to strengthen that.

"Do you want me to take off my pants as well?" He asked, smirking. Of course he was going to be smirking when he had me exactly where he wanted. I couldn't even move. I knew that, if I moved, I would drop the shirt and he would see my shaft and how hard it was right now. I couldn't let him win, no matter how much part of me knew it would be good.

"I don't want you to do anything. It's inappropriate to be without a shirt in my room. You are actually not really that hot."

"So, you're telling me I'm hot?" He asked, undoing his belt and then taking it off. Uh-oh. He wasn't going to go along with this any longer. I wasn't going to allow it.

Or at least, that was what I was telling myself before realizing that, if I rushed toward him, I would be making the biggest mistake of my life. I would have probably dropped the shirt I was holding, and that would have been fatal.

"I'm not telling you that. I'm not actually telling you anything other than that you need to get out of my room before I call the police. As a biker, I'm sure that you don't want the police breathing down your neck."

"No, that would be actually terrible, so I know you're not going to do it."

My mouth continued to water and my scent continued to grow

stronger. Everything that had to be going wrong right now was.

CHAPTER 4

Alix

The truth was that I just really wanted to see his cock and how big it was. For someone so cocky, I knew that it had to be big, but it would still be something different if it was out and pointing at me. I could just imagine his cockhead oozing his pre-come. I felt my mouth watering while thinking about it.

"You want me to do this, don't you?" He asked before I nodded. I knew I shouldn't do that, but I still did.

It happened without my consent. My head just moved on its own. After doing that, he smirked again. And then, Lux took off his belt and lowered his pants. The material moved down slowly as he revealed his underwear. His bulge was exposed. It was plump and big.

Lux also had a boner and my eyes spotted the pool of pre-come forming next to his cockhead. My mind was in such a daze of different thoughts right now. I didn't even know how I should be reacting to this.

My body froze up again, or maybe I should be saying that it had already frozen up a long time ago and I didn't think it would ever go back to its normal state anytime soon.

If before I already had a huge boner, now it was even bigger and was throbbing harder.

He took a couple of steps toward me. He was so close to me

now that I could feel more than just his scent. I could feel the warmth emanating from his body.

"I thought that you were going to be more reluctant about this, but it's obvious that's not the case at all," he said before sneaking his hand under his pair of briefs and then around his dick. My throat was so dry I feared it would never go back to normal.

This was almost too much, and I felt like I was going to pass out.

"On a scale of 1 to 10, how much do you really want to see my shaft right now?" He asked.

The truth was that it was even difficult for me to look up and focus on his eyes. I couldn't do that without hurting the part in me which needed to keep staring at his bulge and boner. Gosh, they were so much bigger than mine that it wasn't even a contest.

"You're not going to answer? That's disappointing," he lamented before lowering his underwear. Black spots showed up in my vision right away, and I really thought I was going to black out, but I actually remained exactly where I was.

His cock was free and out and was pointing right at me. It had to be easily 10 inches long, and who knew how thick. It was also covered with veins, pre-come oozing out. There was also even a big, noticeable vein snaking from the bottom to the top.

I didn't even know why I was staring so much at his shaft. It wasn't like I would suddenly drop to my knees and begin to suck him off. No matter how much part of me wanted to make that happen, I wasn't going to.

Then, without giving me a warning, he took his fingers from around his dick and walked to me. I flinched, thinking that he was going to do the worst imaginable thing to me, but he actually just opened the closet behind me and picked up one of the shirts from a hanger.

While doing that, Lux wasn't even looking at me.

It was the first time he was so close to me that I felt tiny in comparison.

Then, he grabbed one of my pants and even one of my pair of briefs. He held them in front of him while his eyes examined them with care and attention.

His body was as though it had been sculpted by a talented artist. The muscles were mouthwateringly defined and the skin shone under the warm light in the bedroom.

"You know, I think that these clothes don't really fit me," he murmured before putting the clothes back inside the closet. He closed it while I turned around slowly without moving the shirt from over my groin. He wasn't going to see my dick no matter how much he wanted to.

I didn't even know what to say. He did all this just so that he could find out that my clothes didn't fit him? Again, I was certain that Lux was only teasing me.

He turned around slowly before saying, "you're not going to say anything more? Are you really so disappointed with my shaft?"

I almost jumped. I never thought he would be so blunt when making such a question.

"I'm not disappointed about anything!" I barked, immediately covering my mouth while not remembering that I should be holding the shirt in front of my shaft.

I wasn't disappointed with his cock. It was actually pretty impressive and nice, which was why I found his statement so infuriating.

And now, it was too late and he could see my little dick. He could see it entirely and his smirk only widened. He knew that I was slightly submissive, but he never thought that I was such a puny, forgettable Omega.

"There it is. I knew that it wasn't going to take you long to finally drop your shirt." His eyes examined my shaft one more time. "It's actually nice. You don't have anything to be worried about."

"I told you to fucking get out of my room," I growled. I still wanted him to leave me alone.

"I don't think you actually want me to go anywhere, but since you insist so much and I need to leave because I have more important things to do, then that is exactly what I'm going to do," he explained before grabbing my clothes again and putting them on. They were tight on his body, but it was obvious he didn't care about that.

"They are pretty tight, but I think it's fine. Tomorrow, I'll give them back to you," he said before rushing over to the window and then jumping out. I sped to it and grabbed at the frame, watching him as he left while he mounted his motorcycle before turning on the engine and going out the gate. The motorcycle's engine rumbled in the distance while relief washed over me.

So, Lux was gone - for the time being, anyway. I was certain that he would be back and I would be stronger than I was right now.

CHAPTER 5

Alix

Except that being strong wasn't actually my forté. I was back in my bedroom and checking my surroundings while still thinking about Lux. When he was in my bedroom, everything was different.

No matter how much I fought it, he always managed to make me do everything he wanted. He managed to see my cock when I was doing everything not to show it.

That was how persuasive he was. He always had this aura around him which made me feel flustered even though he wasn't even doing anything special.

My cat purred, stepping on the bedspread while I was sitting with my legs crossed on it. I was gazing at Wombat while trying to figure out exactly what was going on in my mind. I always told myself I hated Lux so much, and yet when I had the opportunity to show him that, I failed miserably.

I never thought I would recover from that.

Wombat, lying on his fat belly on the mattress, was the only one who appeared to be interested in hearing what I had to say. His head was resting on his legs and his eyes were closed halfway. He looked bored, no denying it, but he was also the only one around to listen to what I had to say.

"I just don't think that he really is the right one for me. He is always so full of himself that it's maddening."

Wombat craned his head to look at me slowly while showing how bored he was. Even though he couldn't speak, when he yawned, I knew he was trying to tell me something.

Even though you say you hate Lux so much, I don't think that's exactly true. You could really have called the guards on him, but you didn't and I think that says a lot about you.

Maybe I was only imagining things, but I could picture Wombat saying that to me.

Wombat yawned again, stretching his legs.

"You're wrong. It doesn't matter how hot Lux is and that his dick is so big that he would hurt me as much as he would pleasure me, it's still never going to happen."

You can say that as much as you want to yourself, but it's not really going to change the truth. You let him see more of you than you wanted and, in the end, it was fine.

I shook my head. Talking to my cat right now wasn't going to help me with anything, and I actually needed to go back to my studies. I was studying to be a programmer, so that was my focus at the moment.

I jumped off the bed and then turned on my laptop. After loading all the necessary apps and putting my fingers over the keyboard, I prepared myself to make my next program, only to realize that I couldn't.

Something impeded me right now from doing that. It was my mind obsessing over Lux. Now that I was already an adult, I couldn't deny how much my body wanted to be pregnant.

I looked down at my belly and ran my right hand around it, wondering how my life would be if I was pregnant.

I shook my head no more than a second later.

There was no point in wondering about that right now when it just wasn't going to happen.

Despite that, I still found Lux so hot that I couldn't deny I needed to relieve myself somehow right now. So, without thinking about it much more, I rose up from the chair and then sped over to the bathroom. I locked the door and lowered my pants while thinking about Lux. I was fantasizing about him.

No denying it.

That was exactly what was in my mind right now and I was furious. My mind should not be fantasizing about Lux. He didn't even care about me.

But his body was still so perfect, the muscles forming curves that I couldn't find anywhere else or with anyone else for that matter. He knew what he was doing when he showed them to me in my bedroom.

I could imagine him mounting me before sliding his prick inside of me. He would then shoot his come in my tunnel and I would get pregnant with his baby.

Gosh, why was that thought even populating my mind right now? I didn't know, but I still just wanted this moment to end right away.

Maybe I needed to do something crazy. Maybe I needed to go to him and face him head-on before finally telling him how much I hated him.

Then, he would finally stop being so obsessed with me.

But at the moment, I couldn't even work without jacking off while thinking about Lux. His dick was big and veiny, oozing pre-come in my room. If I went back into my bedroom to look for it, I would certainly find his pre-come spot on the floor.

Even though it had already been days since he left during the party, I was certain I could smell his scent in the air. That was how strong it was.

After jacking off and shooting my come into the toilet water, I flushed it while staring at the swirling liquid going down into the drain system.

My balls still ached. This wasn't enough for me. I feared that the only thing that would be enough to quench my arousal at the moment was having sex with Lux. It would never happen, though.

No matter how much part of me wanted it, it just wasn't going to materialize.

CHAPTER 6

Lux

Holding my cigarette between my fingers, I lit up with the flame from my lighter. I put the cigarette on my lips and then I puffed out the smoke while calming down my mind. After everything I went through that night with Alix, I needed this moment where I was in the biker club's building.

It was my safe place. The only place where I could relax and not think about anything while focusing on Alix. I knew I was being a jerk when I took my clothes off in front of him, but it had actually been for a good cause.

He enjoyed everything. He would never admit it, but he liked seeing my body without the clothes. His eyes were dancing left and right and up and down as he took in what his eyes were witnessing.

That was how much he wanted me.

My friend was with me, sitting across from me on the other chair at the table. He was with his arms on the table and was looking at me with attention.

"It's obvious you are still thinking of him, aren't you?" He asked, reclining on the chair he was sitting on.

"It's so difficult for me. Everyone that knows him tells me he wants me to marry him and I want it so much, too, but with the way that he always rejects me, I just can't force myself on him. At least, not without feeling disgusted at myself."

"That's a normal reaction. Don't worry about it, though. I'm sure that he will come around one day."

"You're sure about that? I'm asking that because every time that I was Alix, I think exactly the opposite. It's always a risk, with him possibly calling the police on me. I don't want to bring trouble to the club."

"Don't worry about that. You won't be bringing any trouble to the club. I'm sure that he's only throwing empty threats every time that he brings something like that up."

He chuckled, going with me to the pool sitting by one of the walls in the building. He threw me a cue, which I grabbed mid-air. Then, he positioned the balls on the surface of the pool before lining up the stick to the white ball.

We were playing pool right now, and I was sure I was going to win in this round.

"You really think that? Do you think that I should be more assertive when talking to him?"

After punching the white ball with the stick, he flicked his eyes up, finding my pupils. "How much do you want to marry him? I'm sure that you can't stop thinking about Alix, isn't that right?"

It was true. I couldn't stop thinking about Alix no matter how much I wanted to be doing something different with my life.

Now that I was 30 years old, I just wanted to have an Omega all for myself. One that would have my babies in his belly, and I couldn't do that while Alix was making himself so much harder to me.

"Yeah, it's difficult for me not to be thinking about him. I just want to be with him. I think that he's really amazing. Not to mention that I have this huge crush on him, and my dick gets harder every time I think about him."

I hit the white ball with my stick, throwing a punch in the air to commemorate that I made two balls go into two holes in the pool. Firrol rolled his eyes, groaning.

He just couldn't believe my luck.

But after he returned his attention back to the topic we were discussing, he proposed, "I think that there's actually something I can do to get the truth out of him. I mean, it's obvious that he wants you, but he doesn't want to admit that because you are a biker and also because you are the founder of this club."

That was right. That was one of the main reasons why he said he didn't want to have anything to do with me.

I locked my eyes with his. What exactly was he thinking right now?

"What do you propose?"

"I think that I should leave you in the dark about it."

I widened my eyes.

"What do you mean that you are going to keep me in the dark about something that should actually help me?"

"Just be patient. I'm going to tell you everything – or, rather, you are going to learn everything that I am preparing when the time is right."

When the time was right... I kept thinking about it, and I always came to the same conclusion. I always thought that Firrol was pulling my leg right now, even though he never did that to me before, and I should certainly not be having such thoughts about his intentions.

Groaning, I said, "fine, but I just want a guarantee from you. I want you to promise me that no matter what it is you are planning right now, it's going to work and it's going to be everything I want. I don't usually need help for anything, but since you are my buddy, I'm making an exception."

Firrol hit the white ball on the pool with his stick before straightening his spine. "Don't worry about it. It's all going to work out for you. I've got a good plan in mind."

I smirked. It was the only thing I could do right now. It should be sufficient to make me feel better about this, but it wasn't at that point yet.

I took a deep breath in after realizing that there wasn't much else that could be done.

So, I was probably going to see Alix one more time, and I had no idea what I would say to him when we were together.

Sometimes, even I was lost.

CHAPTER 7

So, here I was. Exactly where was I? I asked myself, thinking that I couldn't see or smell anything thanks to the mask I was wearing. Firrol told me that everything was going to be all right and that he was going to find a way to bring Alix here, but... Was he really going to do that or was this a prank?

Every time that I thought about this, I felt so much more certain about my suspicion.

Even though I couldn't know the exact address where I was, I still knew that it was a moldy room in the middle of nowhere. Or maybe it was just my nose playing tricks on me about that.

I thought I could smell Alix's scent somewhere, but maybe I was just imagining things.

Then, the door to the room where I was opened and I heard footsteps entering. As the Wolf Alpha I was, the first thought that crossed my mind was that it was someone from one of the rival gangs coming to kill me, but then I could kind of make out his scent in the air. It was faint, polluted by the mask, but it was still there.

I knew I wasn't imagining things.

He came to me as he weighed his footsteps. I could hear them echoing on the floor. I could see his mask through my mask. So, this was my friend's idea all along. He paired me with Alix without alerting him to the fact that he was meeting up with me.

After checking my surroundings again, I realized that the room where I was wasn't so bad. It was actually somewhat decent. There was even a bed by one of the walls, where we could lie on.

This was really Alix, and I couldn't be happier about it. Even my cock was showing me the same. It was throbbing and so hard right now while it begged to be put out of my underwear.

Alix snuck his fingers under my shirt. I helped him with lifting it up and over my head. Even if he was anything but his normal self, he had to know that he was with me right now.

Maybe this was his way to combat his fears and limitations. He wanted to have sex with me but not while admitting that he had a huge crush on me. He thought that I couldn't smell his scent. That was silly.

I settled my hands on his shoulders and then I brought him to the bed. But just when he thought that I was going to make him lie down on it, I snuck my fingers under his shirt and then lifted it up. After doing that, I slid my hand over his pecs. They weren't noticeable, but they were still there and I could feel the soft texture of his skin, too.

It was so much softer than mine. After locking my eyes with his through my mask, I lowered my head until my lips were right in front of his nipple. After doing that, I blew a cloud of hot air on it while making his body shudder.

This was finally happening. We were going to have sex and it was going to be amazing for him.

After doing that, I ran my finger around his nipple while focusing on his reactions. His lips parted slightly and I took advantage of the opportunity to lock my lips with his. Even though I was wearing a mask, it didn't cover my entire face.

His lips were incredibly soft.

This was the first time we were kissing, and I couldn't help but slide my tongue inside his mouth. He accepted it. Alix didn't fight back, which was exactly how I was hoping this was going to go. After doing that, we rubbed our tongues against each other, and he let out a breath through his mouth when he realized that I was doing everything right.

We were fucking even though he still thought he didn't know who I was.

After this was over, I would reveal myself to him and he would finally learn the truth. Or maybe not. Sometimes, things were weird in my mind.

After that, I was certain he wouldn't be able to negate how much he wanted me.

We interlaced our fingers while I reached down with my hand before grabbing at his bulge. His erection was already at full mast and he wanted me now inside of him more than anything.

What's more, I didn't stop myself before sliding my fingers under his pair of boxer briefs. He accepted that as well, which only spurred me on to wrap my fingers around his manhood. It was small when compared to mine, but also endearing.

I was going to make him come while he was still with his clothes on. I told him that after locking my eyes with his one more time. He groaned slightly, his eyes looking alarmed. He didn't think that I was going to be so audacious.

But after doing that, he soon calmed down when he realized that this was the best moment in his life in a very long time. Pre-come oozing from the slit in his dickhead, my fingers were already coated with it, and I couldn't be any happier about this.

Pumping his dick over and over, I continued to do what I was doing until he was coming in his pants. His body went stiff and then lost that when he climbed down from his orgasmic high. It was still trembling slightly, though, and I wasted no time before reaching around to cup his asscheek, which I did without showing him anything else.

I then lowered his pants. After this, I had no idea how he would get back home without everyone finding out that he had sex. Given what I knew about him and his background, it was possible this was his first time, in which case I was going to do everything in my power to make sure it was going to be memorable.

My fingers were still enclosed around his little shaft. I wasn't going to let go of it until it was hard again. Even though Alix had just come, it wasn't enough for me.

CHAPTER 8

Alix

There was no denying it. I knew who he was. His body shape, everything about him, his nose, his lips, and, most of all, his scent… it was all so telling. I wasn't with a stranger. In fact, he was the complete opposite of that. I was with Lux. I was having sex with him and I knew that this fact alone should be enough to make me turn back right now, but I couldn't.

The way that he was moving his hands around my body was just too arousing. He was even playing with my nipples, swirling his tongue around them. He knew what he was doing. I was moaning and groaning like never before, and I had just come in my pants. It was the first time something like that ever happened.

I had never been so aroused before in my life.

"Oh fuck, oh fuck," I mumbled over and over when he slid his hand over my abs, feeling the ridges and the curves, rubbing his finger in my belly button as if it wasn't silly. And yet, it kind of wasn't.

After doing that, Lux wasn't satisfied. He needed more. Oh, so much more. And he was so tempting and I was so aroused I couldn't turn back. Even though my mind was begging me to, I just couldn't.

Some seconds later, he decided to slide his hand over my thighs before getting rid of every piece of clothing I had. Gone were my shirt, pants, underwear, socks, and boots. Everything except the mask I still wore.

Lux wasted no time before kissing me one more time. That was like his way to tell me he was not satisfied with what he had already gotten.

Then, he kissed me one more time for good measure before keeping his lips lingering over mine while a line of saliva dangled between them. After that, he peppered my neck with several kisses before moving down and cupping my balls with his right hand.

I threw my head back when he did that. The waves of pleasure that this gave me were enough to hasten my breathing, which only brought a smile to my face. I always knew that having sex was going to be mind-blowing, but I never thought it was going to be so much so.

After this, I had no idea what I would do.

I was so wet right now. Unbelievably so. Lux even ran his finger along my wetness before pulling his hand up and licking his digital clean with his tongue. After doing that, he decided to wrap his lips around my manhood.

Seconds later, I had no idea how much longer I could resist before coming one more time. I didn't want to disappoint him even though I should also be doing everything in my power so that this didn't progress much more than it already was.

A minute later, Lux decided to surprise me by shedding off his clothes. In the blink of an eye, he was naked before me again, but this time, differently from our last encounter, I could relax and bask in the sight my eyes were witnessing.

It was so great.

I could see the curves of his pecs, his pink nipples, and the light fur in the middle of his chest. I drew in a short breath when he came down after moving his hand away from my balls.

He placed his fingers around his manhood and then penetrated me after putting on a condom. I thought that I was going to ride him bareback, and it was such a pity that I couldn't.

But if I could smell his scent, then I was certain he could

also smell mine. The masks we were wearing were supposed to confuse our noses, but they weren't being successful in doing that.

No more than a few seconds later, he went all the way inside of me. Balls deep. I never thought that he would be so deep inside of me, and it came as a surprise to me when I looked down and noticed that there were still some inches that he was unable to fit in there. When Lux was satisfied with the way that I was pressing my walls around his hardness, he started to roll his hips, and I felt his balls slapping against my butt, and it was exhilarating and arousing as much as it was painful.

My ass was already sore from all the beating it was taking, and I knew that it would never be the same again.

He put his fingers under my thighs and then dug them into my skin while pistoning in and out of me as he showed no mercy in his eyes. I could see his pupils behind the mask. Even though it was supposed to cast some shadow over them, it wasn't working.

After my cock started to throb, I came at the same time as he did while he jammed his prick deep inside of me to make sure that I felt as much of his climax as I could.

After that, I collapsed on the bed and he pushed himself away from me before putting on his clothes. I sat up on the bed when I realized he was doing that. I didn't think that he was simply going to walk away after such a jaw-dropping sex with me and taking my virginity.

I would never recover from this in a good way.

I heard him closing the door some seconds after that and then he walked out of the room where I was. There was nothing special about it. It was just a simple, forgettable apartment room in the middle of downtown.

Still, I just had sex with the man I hated the most, and I never thought it would come to this.

Now, how was I going to explain this event to Wombat without looking like a fool?

CHAPTER 9

Alix

The truth was, I couldn't. I opened the door to my room and then I crept over to the bed on my tiptoes. After turning my head left and right, I ascertained that Wombat was nowhere to be seen. He was probably somewhere outside and playing in the sand areas.

It wouldn't be the first time.

After determining that he was nowhere in my room, I took off my clothes. I had already taken off the mask before coming here, so nobody knew that I had been out doing something that would certainly become the main topic of gossip all over the house.

I took a deep breath after shedding off my clothes and then tiptoed to the bathroom before opening the door. After doing that, I turned on the shower head and got under the water.

It was warm and comfortable. The water flowed down my body while washing away the worries in my mind. I kept on worrying that someone was going to discover I was out to have sex with Lux and, if that happened, I wouldn't even know what to say.

I told myself that everything was going to be okay while shampooing my hair. I felt my fingers scrubbing my scalp while my mind remembered the amazing night that I had with Lux. It had been him, right? No denying that it was him. It just wouldn't make any sense otherwise.

After rinsing my hair with lukewarm water, I used body wash on my body. The herbal smell impregnated the air around my nose and I sniffed it, filling my lungs with it.

It was like walking in the clouds.

After doing that, I washed my body with water before stepping out from under the shower head. I dried my body with a towel before going to the sink and checking my reflection in the mirror. Either I was imagining things, or maybe there was something different about it that I couldn't put my finger on.

After losing my virginity, it was like I was someone different, which didn't really make any sense.

I then opened one of my moisturizing creams and just when I was going to spread some of it on my cheeks, I noticed his shadow behind me.

Wombat.

He meowed from behind me while creeping into the bathroom. His tail was high up as he came around me while sliding his body around my legs. He purred, closing his eyes as though he was giving me some support right now instead of judging me, which was welcoming.

"I think I just did the most unimaginable thing that ever happened in my life, buddy."

You had sex with Lux, right? I can see it written all over your face. No matter how much you want to lie to me about it, I know that you went out to do that without telling me about it.

He jumped before landing on the sink in front of me. Then, he put his tail around him while looking up at me with curious eyes. This moment took me out of my reverie so hard that I even forgot that I was supposed to be putting some moisturizing cream on my face.

"You don't need to be so blunt about it."

But I do need to be blunt about it. I have to be your guiding hand because, sometimes, you don't want to do that at all. You always want to pamper yourself as though you are some kind of prince. So, it always falls to me to put you back on the right track.

"That's ridiculous. You are my buddy, but you don't actually have the right-" I shook my head. Here I was talking to my cat again, which would make everyone think that I was going crazy or something like that. And yet, it still spoke volumes about my current life. I was talking to Wombat because he really was my only buddy right now. "And it was a great sex."

He turned around himself, licking his right foot.

I know that it was great. I could see in your eyes how much you've always actually wanted to make that happen. Even though you've always told me that you don't like Lux at all, it has always been nothing more than a lie. I'm happy that you're finally coming to terms with that and maybe from now on, we can move on from this.

I groaned, closing my eyes before putting the facial cream on my cheeks and spreading it on my cheeks with my fingers.

"You know, I don't really need to be judged by now. I thought that you were going to be more okay with what happened."

I'm actually okay with what you did. I just never thought you were going to keep something like that hidden from me.

I sighed, closing my eyes before throwing my shirt on. Maybe I shouldn't have said that to Wombat. He was actually only looking out for me. He was worried about me when I was outside and he didn't have any information about my whereabouts.

After putting on my pants and underwear, I flopped down onto the mattress while Wombat came over to the bed. He jumped and landed on it, resting his head on my right leg.

Again, I'm just happy that you finally accomplished something different in your life. You have been cooped up in your bedroom for so long that I was starting to get worried. And... are you also finally going to tell me how it went?

I blushed. I wasn't going to tell my cat anything about the sex. That would be just weird.

CHAPTER 10

Lux

Alix could possibly think that I was crossing a line by doing this, but he couldn't stop me anymore. After getting his phone number, I decided to contact him. Maybe I was making a mistake, but after that amazing sex we had, I couldn't stop thinking about him.

That was why I was back lying on the bed with my fingers wrapped around my dick. I was thinking about the moment when I finally went inside of him. When that happened, it was like he was on the moon.

My cock ached for more of that. The only problem was that I was certain he didn't want anything to do with me, but... Forget about all that. I wasn't going to be a pussy anymore when it came to Alix.

I had his phone number, so I was going to shoot him a message.

I did that then without thinking about this one more time. It would be a mistake, not to mention that I could still remember how soft his lips were when we kissed.

Me: I know that it was you last night.

I had no idea if he was going to answer me right away, but if he took his time, I was going to be more persistent. After all the goings back and forth with this, it was time for me to take the next step. After all, it wasn't just my mind that was obsessed with Alix, but also my shaft. It was begging to be inside of him again.

Alix: I don't know what you're talking about. As I said, I don't want you to keep bothering me, or else I'm really going to call the police on you and when that happens, I will enjoy seeing you behind bars.

I chuckled. Every time that he brought up the possibility of calling the police on me, I felt like really taking the risk and letting things play out from there.

Me: I know you're not going to do that. When are you finally going to stop being such a pussy and man up?

Alix: it's not working. Nothing that you're doing is working. I certainly didn't have sex with you.

Me: and who said anything about having sex with you? I'm chuckling so much right now. I got you exactly where I needed you. You just confirmed that you really were the one behind the mask.

Alix: I really don't know what you're talking about.

I sighed, rolling over on my back on the mattress while still holding my phone in my hand. My other hand was stroking the skin of my cock slowly and nicely. Not much longer from now and I would be coming all over the bedspread.

Me: do you want to play a little game with me?

I had no idea if he was going to go along with that, but I was hoping that he would. I was hoping that he was finally going to drop the act and begin to play with me a little. After all, it had been one thing seeing him naked while I was wearing that terrible mask on my face, and it would be another if I could see his body in full glory without getting in the way.

Alix: what kind of game?

*Me: see? I knew that you were going to be more malleable with me now. It's a simple game and I know that you can win it without difficulty. I'm going to take you a picture of my cock and you can show me any part of your body that you want. I'm certainly not asking for you to show me your asshole. *Wink**

Alix: as if I'm going to do something like that. If there is something that I learned from my friends, it's that I should never share nudes with anyone.

Me: who said anything about sharing nudes? That's not what this is at all.

Alix: again, I know that you are trying to trick me. It's not going to work.

I groaned, pulling up the phone and opening the camera app. After doing that, I snapped a picture of my dick, which I uploaded to Alix without thinking twice about it. At this point, I was so much more determined than before to show him what he was missing right now. It was what he'd already cherished and loved that other night, so I knew that I was striking gold right now.

I waited and waited and he didn't say anything for the next couple of minutes. *How frustrating this is,* I thought while pulling up my phone and snapping another pic, this time focusing more on my balls. I was sure that someone with Alix's tastes was going to enjoy it as well. After all, his hands were begging to be playing with my balls when we were fucking for the first time.

Me: don't tell me that you don't remember any of this from that night.

Alix: we need to video chat.

My heart jumped in my throat. I never thought that he was going to be so blunt when making such a request. So, he wanted to video chat with me. My balls ached while I thought about that. Oh, we were going to do so much more than just video chat.

Without saying anything else about it, I clicked on the app icon which allowed us to video chat. It took it a while, thanks to my shitty internet connection speed in the motorcycle club, but then there he was... and, wow. I just couldn't believe that I was video chatting with the same guy that threatened me so much with calling the police on me.

The tone on his cheeks didn't lie. He wanted so much to see more of me, especially now that we were sexting.

CHAPTER 11

Alix

I didn't know what I was doing anymore, but it was certainly a mistake. I shouldn't be video chatting with Lux even though I could still remember how I felt when he was inside of me. I'd felt like I was in heaven. And yet, that was in the past.

I couldn't let Lux find out that I enjoyed the sex.

"Nothing of that happened."

"You don't know anything about that. What you are telling me right now is a straight-up lie."

"It's not. I can prove to you that I didn't lose my virginity. You didn't take it."

He chuckled, turning his phone to show me his cock again. Oh, I just knew that he was going to do that.

"You miss this, don't you?" He chuckled, putting his balls in his right hand and then squeezing them gently. His nuts were massive when we had sex. That was something that I remembered well from our night. His hand was just that big.

I blushed even harder than I already was before.

"I don't know what you're saying, and what you're doing is really so inappropriate. You shouldn't be showing your private parts online. Other people could be recording this. I could be recording this so that I could send all this information to the local authorities."

"And yet, you aren't going to do that. What you are going to do right now is to admit that you are the one behind the mask when we fucked."

Fuck. How could I say no to something like that when he was being so persistent?

With my cheeks blushing even harder now than before, I ended up saying, "yeah, it was me. I was the idiot behind the mask. I just wanted to find out what it was like to have sex for the first time."

My heart began to race. For how much longer was I going to keep putting up with this? The truth was that my dick was throbbing right now and in no way could Lux find out about that. If he did, I was certain he would use that against me to force me to marry him.

His eyes widened slightly. What did that mean? That he didn't really believe I was going to tell him the truth so bluntly.

"There it is. The truth. You enjoyed everything, didn't you? If there is something that you are thinking over and over in your mind, it's how good I'm in bed."

"That's not what happened at all. You are putting words into my mouth."

"No, I'm not doing that. What I'm doing is showing you that pretending you hate me isn't exactly what's really going on here. You want me, don't you?" He taunted, his eyes focusing on me. For a moment, I really thought that he was going to show me another snippet of his junk, but he didn't, something that I was thankful for and furious with at the same time. The truth was that his dick was really nice and I could still remember how it felt inside of me. Next time, I would like to feel how it would taste in my mouth. Nothing more than that.

How was I going to respond to that question without betraying everything that I had said up to this point? The truth was that I couldn't.

So, I took a deep breath and prepared to do the worst thing I ever thought I would do in my life.

"I actually don't think that you are amazing in bed."

He chuckled.

"Is there something else that you want to say?"

"Can you please just stop chuckling? It's so maddening and it gets under my skin every single time."

He seemed as though he was going to chuckle again, but he didn't.

"All right, all right. I'm not going to chuckle ever again when we are talking. I'm just happy that you're finally letting behind your pride and admitting that you feel something for me that you can't control."

"So... what's going to happen now?"

With my heart in my throat right now, it was difficult to imagine what would happen now that didn't involve me getting married to him.

And having his babies.

And calling him my husband.

Urgh, every time that I thought about those things, it hurt me. No denying it.

"I want you to come over and meet my buddies."

"Meet your buddies?" I sounded as shocked as I looked. It couldn't be any different. I never thought that I would go to his motorcycle club, but it was still happening.

"I want to show you that we are actually decent people. You can understand why I'm doing this, don't you?"

I looked up while stroking my dick under my pants. My mind suddenly thought of Wombat. Even though he was nowhere to be seen right now, I was sure that he was either overhearing this or would find out about what I was talking about with Lux sometime later.

Plus, this could be a chance to fuck Lux again. Then, I would finally tell him the truth about my feelings for him. I knew that it would be a mess and it would all come tumbling out of my mouth, but it would still be better than pretending that I hated him.

"Looking at it that way, I can see your point. I'm going there to your motorcycle club and you're going to show what it's like to me, and I'll try to swallow my pride."

"Perfect, but..." He took a deep breath, making me brace for whatever else he was going to say. "This is still not over. Now that you've just admitted that you want me as much as I want you, how about finally snapping me a photo of your little pink asshole? After all, I still remember how I felt when I was inside of it."

I gulped but still did as he asked. If he wanted to see my orifice so much, then he was going to get it.

CHAPTER 12

Alix

I had to admit that I never thought I would be riding on his motorcycle and that he was going to take me to his motorcycle club so that he could show me that his buddies were actually more decent than I thought.

I climbed onto his motorcycle before putting my arms around him. His body was still as massive and arousing as the first time that I touched it. That night when we were together, I was able to run fingers all over the curves of his pecs, abs, biceps, and pretty much every other part of his body.

His cologne wafted in the air while my nose sniffed it. I imagined that it wasn't common for a biker to spray perfume on his body for any occasion, but he did before coming to my house.

"This doesn't mean that we are going to get married or anything like that," I pointed out right away. It was better to make sure that he understood me and where I stood between how things were currently going between us.

"Sure, no problem," he said while smirking. Of course he was going to be smirking at that. At least, he didn't chuckle like I thought he was going to.

After placing his fingers around the handles of the motorcycle, the engine roared to life when he rode off. We were both wearing helmets, so there was no reason to be worried about anything, even though I soon noticed that he was already speeding and going through the red lights.

"Hey, you shouldn't be doing this!" I shouted over the loud noise of the motorcycle's engine. Between that and the helmet he was wearing, I doubted that he could hear me, but I still insisted on trying.

"Fine, fine. Sometimes, Alix, you are no fun," he grumbled before slowing down the motorcycle. I could still feel the engine rumbling under my butt, which was frightening, albeit only slightly. This was better.

I just hoped that he wasn't going to notice my boner under my pants. If he did, I was certain that he would use that to his advantage again. There were so many things about me that he could do for that purpose.

"Enjoying riding on my motorcycle with me so far?" He asked while looking over his shoulder and focusing his eyes on me. My arms were around his torso, so I could feel, now much more than ever before, the warmth emanating from it. It was welcoming and comforting in a way I never thought possible. It made me want to lower my hand and find his cock, and it was a pity that I couldn't do that without betraying the last vestiges of my true being.

"So, so," I responded. I wasn't going to say just how much I was actually enjoying riding on his motorcycle. How could I do that without feeling like I betrayed myself?

The truth was that I couldn't, so I was focusing on doing the right thing for now.

Still, my erection was on the verge of being noticeable and he could almost feel it as well.

"That's disappointing. I really thought that you were going to connect with this and you were going to realize that riding on a motorcycle actually isn't that bad."

I groaned. No matter what Lux told me, it wasn't going to change my mind. I was only doing this so that I could show him that we actually didn't have anything in common and, after he realized that, he would say that he didn't want to marry me anymore. I didn't even know why people thought that pairing me with a biker was a good idea. It was so mind-boggling.

Some seconds later, he pulled up by the front of the motorcycle club. With broken windows and graffiti on the walls, it wasn't the kind of place where I wanted to find myself right now. I was much more respectable and I deserved to be spending my time in a place where I didn't feel disgusted with everything.

I took a deep breath in after realizing that there was nothing else that could be done about this. Lux put his hand on my right shoulder and then he pushed me slightly until I was walking inside the building with him. He opened the door for me and I soon found myself in the main room – or at least, what I was assuming to be the main room – and then he waved his hand over his head to capture the attention of someone in the distance.

A handful of bikers populated the club and they were doing different activities together, like playing cards, chatting, drinking, and smoking. Again, I felt disgusted with what my eyes were witnessing.

I turned around as I said, "I really shouldn't be in this place. It's not for me."

"Come on, I said that I was going to show you around and introduce you to my buddies, so that's exactly what I'm going to do," he insisted while keeping his hand on my shoulder and making me walk until we were no more than a couple of feet in front of a member of the motorcycle club.

"He is the vice president of the club, and I'm the founder and the president of it," Lux explained while putting his arm around me. It was like he was doing this so that I had no chance to escape. "His name is Firrol."

Firrol. I was going to keep that name in mind, I thought while his eyes examined me with the utmost attention. I felt so out of place in this building. Even the other bikers were staring at me with judging eyes. They were most likely asking themselves what someone like me, who looked so pompous and clean, was doing here.

To be honest, I was asking myself that, too.

CHAPTER 13

Lux

"So, did you like meeting my buddies?" I asked, my arm positioned on the wall in my room while he wrung his hands. He didn't need to look so uncomfortable with being here, but he still did.

"Yeah, I supposed that they are actually nice people."

"See? I told you that you were going to convince yourself that there is actually nothing really that bad in my life and the fact that I am a member of a motorcycle club."

"I still don't like that you are the founder of it. That means that, if we ever got married, I would have to come here often and I would have to interact with your buddies."

I sighed. Was it really going to take that to convince him that we could live together without the biker part of my life getting in the way? Sometimes, that was exactly what I thought.

"There is actually something that I need to tell you about that."

He perked up. "What is it? Tell me everything."

"I'm going to leave the motorcycle club. If it takes that to convince you that you actually love me more than you hate the biker part of my life, then I see no problem with leaving all this behind."

He widened his eyes in the same instant.

"No, you don't need to do that. Not because of me. You like all this, so if this is what you want to do with your life, then, by all means, don't change it because of me."

I placed my hand under his chin. After tilting his head up and locking my eyes with his, I affirmed, "this is actually what I want to do. I want to kiss you one more time. I want to feel how soft your lips are again."

Alix's eyes were trembling slightly. What was he thinking right now? I could only wonder.

"You are actually willing to do that because of me?" He asked while nearing his head to mine.

"Yeah, I'm thinking about doing that. It's how much I really want to marry you."

Then, we connected our lips. They were unbelievably soft just like we kissed that time, and I couldn't focus on anything else right now that wasn't extending this kiss for as long as possible.

But even this wasn't enough. I need to do so much more, which was why I lowered my hand while looking for his hard-on. It was already poking against his pants. He moaned when I put my hand against it and pressed him slightly against the wall behind him.

After doing that, it was only natural that we ended our kiss, though only for now.

"So, have I finally convinced you that we can be together and you don't have to be thinking about the fact that I'm a biker? After all, if you say yes, then I'm going to leave all this behind."

Alix cleared his throat while lowering his hand and before putting it under my shirt. His fingers danced over my abs while he smiled gently. It was almost not there, but it still was.

"You actually don't need to leave your buddies behind. I want to be with you. Even though it doesn't make sense after everything that I've said to you, I think that I really want to marry you," he admitted before lifting my shirt and revealing, to the delight of his eyes, my defined, chiseled chest.

The way that he was looking at it was telling. He enjoyed what his eyes were seeing. His mouth was dry thinking about licking, kissing, and doing everything else that he could while he enjoyed every other part of me.

I couldn't help but close the door behind me so that nobody interrupted us. After doing that, I rushed over to him before stripping him off his clothes. No better time than now to love and worship the softness of his skin. I was already doing that while he threw his legs around me.

After doing that, Alix started to grind his body against mine while rubbing his dick against mine. I could feel it trembling under the way that I was dominating him right now.

Given that he was already at a disadvantage, I decided to do something about that before getting rid of my clothes as well. It all happened so fast that I didn't even know how we went from discussing if I would ever marry him to fucking him again.

The best thing about this was that we were doing this while not being worried about how much he didn't actually want to do this even though it was a lie.

Some seconds later, I moved down before wrapping my lips around his gland. It was already vibrating and oozing his pre-come. After licking my tongue around it and coating it with it, I decided to do something we didn't do when we fucked for the first time.

I did the unimaginable while moving up and lining up my shaft to his mouth. It was already so open and willing for this. After I lowered my hips, my cock went inside his mouth with very little resistance while he was still lying on the mattress.

The only thing that was nagging me right now was that I couldn't go all out without the other bikers finding out about this. We all respected each other's privacy, so I couldn't be as relentless as I wanted to be right now.

Still, I couldn't stop myself before pounding in and out of his mouth while holding back the urge to come all inside of it. I knew that he was thinking the same thing and that he was most likely obsessed with that, given the way that his eyes were beginning to get teary and the lust that covered them, which only made this feel a little bit underwhelming.

Well, I wasn't going to let that get in the way, so I kept on thrusting in and out of his mouth without making him gag. Me being an Alpha, it was impossible for me not to feel my dick enlarging when I noticed that it was nearly the right moment to shoot out my load.

But it wasn't going to happen, and certainly not right now. I wasn't going to do anything that could disappoint Alix after he confirmed everything to me.

ALIX'S EPILOGUE

It wasn't enough that he was fucking my mouth with so much vigor right now. I needed more. I needed so much more that I didn't stop myself before grabbing at his balls and playing with them. They were pulsing with the warmth emanating from his body.

They were also lovingly textured and I could even feel the ridges under my fingers. After moving my fingers between his nuts, though, it became obvious to me that he wanted to do something else. Lux then pulled out, which was disappointing, but not at all unexpected.

After pulling out, he decided to move his hands over my thighs while kneading the skin. The way that he was doing that was incredibly arousing and I could feel waves of arousal pumping through my body. My breathing quickened when he wasted no time before turning me around and licking my asshole with his fingers. It was already wet and begging for him to penetrate it, which I knew he was going to do in a moment.

But even just turning and rubbing his fingers inside of me wasn't enough. Lux needed to do something more, which he did the moment when he felt that the time was right for this. He bent down before sticking his tongue out and licking around my orifice. The way he did that sent waves of pleasure through my body, which all accumulated in my gland.

Fearing that I was going to come and disappoint him before the time was right, I decided to surprise him by pinching my mushroom-shaped cockhead. After widening his eyes, Lux softened them before lining up his prick to my waiting orifice.

He pressed it against it before easing it in without any difficulty. Before long, he was already fully inside of me and this was happening without him using a condom. He just didn't want to ruin this moment that we were sharing. Lux wanted to be inside of me bareback and to feel as much of me as he could.

And it was working. I could feel his massive rod inside of me getting even bigger while he rolled his hips. His balls slapping against my but, slapping sounds filled the room, and I hoped that the walls were thick enough to muffle most of the noise we were making.

Moments before erupting and unloading his sperm inside of me, which would essentially make me pregnant with his baby – or perhaps even many babies – he stopped rolling his hips to make sure that not even a single drop of his come was going to be wasted.

After that, we both collapsed on the bed when he wrapped his arms around me and cocooned me in them. Moments later, he whispered into my right ear, "I love you so much and I can't live without you."

LUX'S EPILOGUE

It was difficult for me not to be with Alix all the time after he revealed how much he loved me. I told him that and I was the first one that did it, but it was when he confirmed it to me that I truly felt we were in love and that nothing could ever separate us.

Was I still a member of the Alpha MC? Sure, I was, and I was also still the founder. Nothing behind that would ever change, especially now that Alix confirmed everything to me. He was okay with the development of our life.

After determining that he was okay with me being a biker, we decided to move and live somewhere that wasn't his old house and we could have a place that wasn't so vast. After all, we both didn't want to start to pay for housekeepers, groundskeepers, maids, butlers, and the like. We just didn't have the time and the money for that, not to mention that we both appreciated having more privacy.

After doing that, we bought everything we were going to need, including all the furniture pieces for the baby's room. That's right. He was pregnant with my baby. It was now three months after we found out about the pregnancy, and Alix could never hide the smile that always appeared on his face whenever the topic was mentioned.

"I'm just so happy that we are together," I cooed when he walked out of the shower box and I wrapped my arms around him. After pressing my groin against his butt, I lowered my hand while looking for his hard-on. I knew that his prick was rock-hard, so

I felt energized to go on with this. When my fingers were going around it, my mouth watered while kissing the nape of his neck over and over again so that he always remembered how this felt.

His dick was oozing pre-come, so I was loving this even more. It was warm and sticky, and I just loved the way that it flowed around my fingers. He groaned after closing his eyes and I continued to pump his dick for what felt like hours until he finally began to come all over the floor in the bathroom. His body began to tremble and shake violently, but he didn't go anywhere because my arms were tightly locked around him.

After this was over, he turned around before throwing his arms around me and then we connected our lips the moment he said over and over again "I just love you so much, but I don't think that this is really just about love. I want to feel you inside of me right now, and there's nothing and no one that can stop us. Also, since we are living alone this time, we can do anything and everything we want without having to worry about what other people would think."

He was right about that. My hand was already going around his body and I wasted no time before cupping his asscheek. It was smooth and so soft. I just couldn't have enough of it, especially now that we were going to fuck.

The moment was right for that.

"And I love you so much that I know that you just read my mind. It's exactly what I want to do, too."

Love.

Sex with my loved one.

What more could an Alpha ask for?

The End

If you are looking for more books like this one, then don't forget to check out these stories

1. Omega for Obsessive Alpha

2. Omega for Protective Alpha

3. Omega for Jealous Alpha

Don't forget to leave your review. It really helps me!

TEASER: OMEGA FOR OBSESSIVE ALPHA

Wolf Shifter MPREG Fated Mates Romance (Omegaverse MC - 1)

Feran

I felt something sniffing me, like he was trying to smell me. I cracked open my eyes as I found someone standing right in front of me. It was a man, huge, older than me, and hot as balls. The moment my eyes set on him, it was like fireworks exploded in my head.

I wanted to rip his clothes off his body and see what he was like naked. I wanted to slide my tongue over his muscles, to feel him for the man he was, to grind my body against his, and to make sweet love with him. I was already drooling even though I didn't even notice that yet.

The guy who was in front of me was so close I could smell the minty odor coming out of his mouth. His eyes were emerald green, his hair messy and blond, some stubble on his chin. His face was chiseled and followed hard lines, making me want to put my hand on it and feel it until he was smiling.

And I just noticed I was supposed to be falling to the floor.

I felt something holding me in place so that that didn't happen. It was his arm, wrapped around my torso. It was firm, showing off his confidence. I was still in the same room from before, which was behind the bar where I was drinking away my sorrows.

I just remembered something terrible that happened not too long ago, which made me come running to this place. I supposed I should be thankful he was holding me like this so that I didn't fall and hurt myself, but the way he was smelling me was also frightening and annoying. I should be shoving him away from me as fast as possible and as hard as I could, but that was easier said than done.

I wasn't going to say that I was skinny. In fact, I was lean and I did work out, but I didn't follow any diet and I didn't inject my body with anything. This guy, on the other hand, looked more like a gym rat than anything.

And he was even more frightening because his body was covered in tattoos. There was even one of them, which caught my attention the most, sneaking from under his shirt and going across his neck. It was the tattoo of a lone wolf, making me remember that he was probably from *that* MC gang. I shivered at the thought of having caught the attention of one of them. It was the worst thing that could be happening.

Not to mention that I didn't have anything to do with him...

He parted his lips, blowing a bigger cloud of his mouth's odor over my face. I closed my eyes and scrunched up my nose, but not because I was turned off by the smell, but because his scent was overwhelming.

As an Omega, I was always subjected to this kind of situation, especially when the other guy was an Alpha. And it wasn't just the smell coming out of his mouth that was making me hard and aroused right now. It was also his musky scent, which came from all around his body.

"I just saved you from hurting yourself. I think you should be thanking me." And as soon as he finished saying that, he smiled, showing me his perfect teeth. I always thought that bikers like him didn't brush their teeth, but it looked like he was an exception.

I knew he was a biker because of the patch he had on the front of his leather jacket. It showed that he, indeed, was from one of the biker gangs in the region. They were called the Wolf Bikers, and everyone around here in the city feared them. They were a menace, robbing people and their houses, causing the police all sorts of troubles.

I knew that coming to this bar was a mistake, but I didn't think I was going to run into a member of the Wolf Bikers.

I shot my hands to his chest, shoving them against it. I thought he was going to leave me alone and add some distance between us, but he held his ground, tightening how hard his arm was pressing against my torso...

Yel

I stomped hard onto the grass, my fangs growing bigger. Fisting my hand, I couldn't help but feel like punching that bear biker until blood was gushing out of his mouth. I was going to bash his head against the pavement until his skull cracked, I swore.

I couldn't believe I was so amateur about it. I should have realized someone was going to come after him, too. I was going to make bank by kidnapping Feran.

Stomping on the grass again, all I could do was turn back and stride over to Delight, my bike. It was parked in front of the bar. The members of the Wolf Bikers didn't know that I was here. They didn't frequent this part of town. I was the only one here, and the only one who should have known about Feran.

He was from one of the most important families in the city. I knew that kidnapping him would make me a lot of money. I didn't even feel bad about it, and I wouldn't either way. The money his family would have to hand over wouldn't even dent their fortune, after all.

I couldn't lose this opportunity.

The moon high above the buildings and the houses, I looked up at it as I realized how easy it would have been to turn into a wolf while that Bear Biker was pointing his gun in my direction. In a fair fight, did he think he would win?

Fuck that guy. He'd always been a nuisance. He was keeping tabs on me.

Ennith…

I was going to punch his gut so hard one day he would puke whatever was in his stomach, I swore, swinging my leg over Delight and remembering all the things that happened between us. All the clashes we had, even when he was in school and trying to prove to the teachers he was better than me at pretty much anything. He joined up with the Bears because they were the right fit for him.

Turning on the engine of the motorcycle and propelling it forward, crossing one red traffic light after the other without even putting on my helmet, I was focused on just one thing – finding Ennith and Feran. I was pretty sure I knew where he was taking him to.

The Bear Bikers' hideout.

It wasn't too far and even though I wasn't going to have the support of the Wolf Bikers, I should be okay. I didn't need them, anyway. I was pretty confident in how well I could sneak in and out of that place. It was pretty big, with ample free space. I was going to have to keep my guard up all the time, but it wasn't a challenge impossible to tame.

I smirked, feeling overconfident. I had my gun with me now. I'd left it in the motorcycle because I didn't think I was going to have to use it during the kidnapping. I thought it was going to be simple. Feran was pretty small, a little lean, weak, and very submissive. Me being the Alpha I was, he was always going to smell me and fall to his knees when his nose got a sniff of it. I mean, everything was going according to plan before Ennith popped up.

I couldn't help but feel aroused by Feran, though. He had short, dark hair, perfect lips, ocean-blue eyes, and lips that were just the right size. When I enclosed my arm around his torso, the first thought that popped up in my mind was how much I wanted to rip the clothes off his body and bend him over. It only didn't happen because raping was something I would never do.

He was about 10 years younger than me, too. That was a piece of information I dug out on the internet. And that age gap was a plus for me, too. If we had met under different circumstances, I'd be going for him for sure. The only problem with that was that now he thought of me just as an asshole who was trying to kidnap him.

Being the person I was, I couldn't care less about that.

I pulled up not too far from their hideout, pushing my motorcycle until it was hidden in a dark and forgotten alleyway between two massive buildings. I pulled up my hood, shadowing my face, and went to one of the doors that two guards were by the side of.

Their hands went to their pistols as soon as they realized someone was padding over to them...

MPREG SERIES AND MORE

SERIES - PREGNANT FOR HIM

1. Controlled by the Alpha 1: An MPREG Omegaverse Story
2. Controlled by the Alpha 2: An MPREG Omegaverse Story
3. Controlled by the Alpha 3: Dominating the Fertile Omega
4. Controlled by the Alpha 4: An Omega's Tale of Obedience
5. Controlled by the Alpha 5: A Tale of Obedient Submission
6. Controlled by the Alpha 6: Monopolized in Outer Space

SERIES - LOST INNOCENCE

1. Overwhelming the Omega 1: His Little Doll
2. Overwhelming the Omega 2: Brute Entry and Double Teamed
3. Overwhelming the Omega 3: His Tight Backdoor
4. Overwhelming the Omega 4: Stretching his Front Door
5. Overwhelming the Omega 5: Until he Spasms
6. Overwhelming the Omega 6: Naïve and Untouched

Straight to gay first time bundles:

1. Stuffed by Blue Collars: The Full Straight to Gay Age Gap Story

2. Throbbing Hard: A Straight to Gay MMF Bundle

3. Teasing Older Men: 16 Straight to Gay MM Stories

4. Helping Hand: 13 Forbidden Older Man Stories

5. So BIG It Hurts MEGA Bundle: 14 Stories of Man of the House, Brats and Gay Sitters

ABOUT THE AUTHOR

Steamy MM stories, baby! Michael Levi can't go a day without sitting down and putting into words all the dirty scenes that sprout in his mind. His collection is diverse, but it's gay love only. And if you are looking for something free, check his mailing list. Warning: it can be extra spicy.

When Michael Levi isn't writing, he's chilling out by the lake close to his house. Nothing better than kicking back with a martini in his hand as he daydreams his next explicit scenes.